This is a first edition published in 2019 by Flying Eye Books,
an imprint of Nobrow Ltd. 27 Westgate Street, London E8 3RL.

Written by Stephen Davies and illustrated by Seaerra Miller,
based on the characters and storylines created
by Luke Pearson and Silvergate Media company.
HILDA™ © 2019 Hilda Productions Limited,
a Silvergate Media company

Published in the US by Nobrow (US) Inc.

Printed in Poland on FSC® certified paper.

ISBN: 978-1-912497-79-9

Order from www.flyingeyebooks.com

Based on the Hildafolk series of graphic novels by Luke Pearson

HILDA
AND THE GREAT
PARADE

Written by Stephen Davies   Illustrated by Seaerra Miller

FLYING EYE BOOKS
London | New York

CONTENTS

A clock ticked. A fly buzzed. Hard chalk squeaked
on a dry chalkboard. Hunched on a wooden bench,
a little girl with blue hair sat in the classroom with
her cheek on her chin, gazing out of the window at
the skyscrapers in the city centre.

"Hilda!" called Miss Hallgrim. "WHAT is so
INTERESTING out there?"

Hilda blinked and turned to look at her teacher.
Miss Hallgrim had a square jaw, stern eyes and
a mass of white hair that made her look as if she
was glaring out from the middle of a cloud.

"Interesting, Miss? Nothing, Miss," said Hilda.

Isn't that the truth? she thought. Nothing interesting out there and nothing interesting in here. Nothing interesting in all of Trolberg. Not like my old home in the wilderness, where there were mountains to climb, caves to explore and all sorts of magical creatures to befriend...

"What was I SAYING, Hilda?" Miss Hallgrim demanded. She had an alarming habit of making her voice go suddenly loud and then quiet again.

"You were saying..." Hilda shielded her eyes and squinted sideways at her neighbour Frida's exercise book. One of the reasons that Frida was top of the class was that she made copious notes on everything Miss Hallgrim said. "You were saying that the Great Parade is three days from now. It is the most special day of the year in Trolberg and our class has been chosen to decorate a stoat for the parade."

The class sniggered. Hilda peered more closely at Frida's handwriting. "A float!" she cried, too late.

"Not a stoat, a float. Like a carnival float.

No one decorates stoats. That would be dumb. They don't even stay still."

Laughter rang in Hilda's ears. Not kind laughter but the sort of cruel, mocking laughter that she had heard so many times in class these last two weeks. Hilda's cheeks burned and she lowered her head so that her blue hair fell in curtains on both sides of her face.

"SILENCE," said Miss Hallgrim frostily. "Hilda is correct, we are going to decorate a FLOAT. In addition, we shall prepare an EXHIBITION for your parents to come and look at. You will work together in groups of three to collect FASCINATING objects on the theme of" – she turned to write on the board – "WONDERFUL TROLBERG."

Hilda snorted. She didn't mean to snort. The sound burst out of her nose all by itself as soon as she heard Miss Hallgrim say 'Wonderful Trolberg'. If ever there were two words that didn't fit together, it was those two.

Miss Hallgrim whirled round. "Has a TROLL

wandered into our classroom or did that DISGUSTING noise come from one of YOU?"

"Sorry, Miss," said Hilda, raising her hand. "It won't happen again."

"You're right, Hilda, it won't," Miss Hallgrim said. "Because you will be standing outside in the CORRIDOR until the HOME TIME BELL."

Hilda stood in the corridor, fuming. Why did the teacher not like her? she wondered. Was it because she asked Miss Hallgrim too many questions, or was it because she hardly ever accepted Miss Hallgrim's answers?

The bell rang suddenly, making Hilda jump. That was another thing about Trolberg. Wherever you went there was always some sort of bell ringing or bonging or trilling or donging.

The classroom door burst open and Trevor and his friends rushed out. Trevor was the class bully and he seemed to have taken a strong dislike to Hilda.

"Look who it is, guys!" Trevor said. "It's the stoat

decorator! Hey, Stoat Girl, tell us again why you moved to Trolberg?"

"Our cabin in the wilderness got stepped on by a giant," said Hilda in a small voice.

"Stepped on by a giant!" Trevor cackled. "I'll never get tired of hearing that. Catch you later, Stoat Girl!" With that, he gave Hilda a stinging flick on the ear and sprinted off down the corridor.

Frida and David were next out. Hilda had seen David around the place but she had hardly ever spoken to him, other than to tell him he had a bug on his head, which he usually did.

"You've got a bug on your head," said Hilda now.

"Thanks." David reached up to brush it off.

Frida looked at Hilda. "Why did you say *stoat* instead of *float?*"

Hilda shrugged. "Your f's are too curly. They look like s's."

"No, they don't! My f's have just the right amount of curliness. Not to mention crossbars. Now get your bag and come with us."

"What? Come where?"

"To the Gorrill Gardens bell tower," said Frida, passing her a pair of binoculars. "We need to get up high and scour the land for interesting plants to take cuttings from."

"Why do we need plant cuttings?"

"For the Wonderful Trolberg exhibition, of course. Miss Hallgrim put us all in threes and you're with me and David here. We've already talked about it, and we've decided we're going to do a 'plants of Trolberg' exhibit."

"Actually, it was Frida who decided that," said David. "I couldn't get a word in edgeways."

"Balderdash," said Frida. "You were nodding the whole time. Now, Hilda, hurry up and get your school bag. We need to be at the top of that bell tower before the sun sets, or we won't see any plants at all."

2

Hilda bounded up the bell tower, taking the spiral steps two at a time. When she came out through the trapdoor at the top, the view made her gasp out loud. Mount Halldór towered in the east, Mount Hár in the west. Stretching all the way down to Björg Fjord, hundreds of rooftops glowed in the afternoon sun between the snow-capped peaks.

A few minutes later David and Frida arrived too, puffing and panting and leaning on each other for support.

"One hundred and twenty-five steps," David wheezed. "Where on earth did you learn to climb so fast, Hilda?"

"I've been climbing all my life," said Hilda. "Mountains. Wind turbines. Troll rocks. Waterfalls. When I lived in the wilderness with my mum, I used to pack my satchel with sketchbooks and cucumber sandwiches and head out on long adventu—"

"Wait a second." David lowered his voice to a whisper. "Did you just say *troll rocks*?"

"I'm afraid so." Hilda giggled. "Once, I was sitting on one, on its nose, when the sun went behind a cloud. The troll came to life and chased me through the Great Forest and then it reached down and grabbed me round my waist, lifting me up to its gaping, drooling—"

"What an incredible story," said Frida. "I'd love to hear it some time."

Hilda fell silent. "Some time" clearly meant "not now". As for David, he was so pale with fright he was practically see-through. Hilda went to the rail and gazed at the high walls that surrounded the city of Trolberg, walls that had been built to keep out not just trolls but anything else that was wild or mysterious or interesting.

"Let's get to work," said Frida, unfolding a big map of Trolberg. "You two scan the city for interesting plants and bushes, and I'll mark the locations on this map."

David lifted his binoculars to his eyes. "Clumps of crabgrass down there by the church," he said. "And lots of purple thistle along the riverside."

"Good work," said Frida, marking the locations on her map with a sharp pencil.

"Patch of yellow behind the grocer's shop," said David. "Unless I'm much mistaken, those are dandelions!"

"Well done, David," said Frida. "Hilda, why do you keep doing that thing with your eyebrows? Do you not understand the task?"

"Sorry," said Hilda, "but I thought you wanted

interesting plants and bushes. Crabgrass, purple thistle and dandelions aren't interesting. They're literally everywhere."

"Is that so?" Frida's voice was cold. "And what would you call an interesting plant, O Great Explorer?"

"Burping bugtrap," Hilda answered. "Its flowers look like grinning mouths. The flowers eat beetles and then burp out loud."

David lowered his binoculars and gaped at Hilda in horror.

"And giant rofflewort," continued Hilda. "I call it the Hide-and-Seek Flower because it has a massive hole in the middle, big enough to hide in. And you'd love the gyrating geraniums on Boot Mountain, Frida. Big red flowers that dance when you sing to them. And the scurvygrass on cliff faces is strong enough to swing on. And nila grass, of course, which shrivels up when you touch it."

"OK," said Frida. "Perhaps we should get back to—"

"No, wait, there's more," said Hilda. "We all know what moss looks like, but have you ever seen moss with LEGS?"

Frida held up a hand to stop her. "That's enough," she said. "Listen, Hilda, I'm sorry if our city seems boring to you, but we've got a job to do here, and we can't take cuttings of plants that don't even grow in Trolberg. So, you can either help us out with this map or you can skedaddle off back to your burping roffle-woffles and your giant scurvylegs and your ... your..."

"Blue nettle," said Hilda.

"Exactly."

"No, I'm saying I can see some blue nettle right over there." Hilda lowered her binoculars and pointed to a tiny fleck of blue at the foot of Mount Hár.

Frida looked, then frowned. "That's miles away," she said.

"Nonsense," said Hilda. "It's inside the city wall, isn't it?"

"Only just," said David. "And you can see for yourself how ancient and crumbly the wall is. If a troll really wanted to get through, it would have no problem at all."

"Come on, guys," Hilda persisted. "Blue nettle is incredibly rare. We'd be sure to get bonus points if we had blue nettle in our exhibit."

Frida took the binoculars and gazed at the blue nettle. "I don't know," she murmured.

"If you're worried about getting stung," said Hilda, "don't be. Blue nettle is not like green nettles. It doesn't sting. Some people actually eat it."

"Really?"

Hilda nodded eagerly. "It's supposed to be good for your brain. Just think of that, Frida. You could chew a leaf or two before the end of term tests, to help you remember all those lovely facts you've learned."

That did the trick. Frida's eyes lit up and she marked on her map the location of the blue nettle. "We'll go tomorrow after school," she said.

A sudden clang from the colossal bell above their heads made Hilda nearly jump out of her skin. Hilda knew that the purpose of the bell towers was to keep trolls away from the city. Trolls hated the sound of bells and Hilda knew exactly how they felt.

"Look down there," said David, pointing. "It's Trevor and his gang."

Hilda looked. At the foot of the bell tower was Gorrill Gardens, a very grand name for a very ugly spot. Gorrill Gardens contained nothing but a few spindly elm trees, a rusty climbing frame and two broken swings.

Trevor and his friends were pacing around the park filling their pockets with stones and pebbles. Hilda's first thought was that they must be doing a rock collection for their Wonderful Trolberg exhibit. But then Trevor approached a flock of birds perching in a nearby elm tree and flung a stone at them.

"Stop!" yelled Hilda.

The birds rose into the air with squawks

of outrage, but Trevor just laughed and threw another stone. His friends threw theirs too, and soon the air was filled with stones and feathers and cruel laughter. Most of the stones missed their mark, but one did not. A little raven dropped out of the elm tree and landed on the ground with a sickening thud.

"I win!" cried Trevor.

"You beast!" shrieked Hilda from the top of the bell tower.

She ran to the trapdoor, hopped down onto the spiral banister and began to slide down it. Faster and faster she slid, leaning back against the wall to balance herself. She shot off at the bottom and cannoned out into the park, yelling and waving, a white-hot ball of rage.

Hilda pushed past Trevor and flung herself down next to the stricken bird.

"Raven, are you OK?" she gasped.

A wing tip twitched. The raven opened a beady eye.

"Thank heavens, you're alive!" cried Hilda. "I do hope you're not hurt."

The raven coughed. "I'm fine," it said.

Hilda gasped. She had never met a talking bird before, not even in the wilderness. She scooped up the raven in both hands and let it nestle against her woollen jumper.

Trevor stared. "Did that bird just talk?" he said.

"No." Hilda turned her back on him and began to walk away.

"Did anyone else hear that?" Trevor asked. His friends shrugged and shook their heads. "It talked," Trevor insisted. "I swear it did. Let me see it."

Hilda broke into a run. "You'll have to catch me first!" she shouted.

She sprinted through the streets of Trolberg, cradling the raven. She crossed the river at

the Bronstad Lane footbridge and ran past the library with Trevor in hot pursuit. Hilda was a fast runner, but she was finding it hard to run at full speed whilst carrying the bird, and Trevor seemed to be gaining on her with every step.

The Trolberg steam train was approaching the city from the south, belching clouds of grey-white smoke. Hilda dashed towards the railway crossing gates, scrambled up the embankment and leaped across the track only seconds before the gates

came down. She just got through before the train roared over the crossing. The driver looked shocked and shook his fist in rage as Hilda charged down the other side of the embankment, past the Scout Hall and into a maze of terraced houses. She stole a glance behind her and saw that Trevor was no longer following – he was trapped on the other side of the passing train.

"That was absolutely terrifying," said the raven.

"I know," grinned Hilda. "Great, wasn't it?"

Left and right and right again, Hilda raced through the streets. When she had first arrived in Trolberg, all these streets had looked exactly the same, but now she was beginning to notice differences. Different styles of lamp post, different shapes of chimney, different coloured timber on the faces of the houses. Even in a dirty, dull city like Trolberg it was possible to find one's way around.

Ten minutes later, they arrived at the apartment block where Hilda lived. She ran up three flights of steps, took out her door key and let herself into Flat 5. There was a cold draught in the flat and a strong smell of wet paint.

Hilda shut the door behind her and hid the raven under her jumper.

"Is that you, dearest?" Mum called from the living room.

"Yes!" called Hilda. "Hi, Mum!"

"Hi, Mum!" croaked a voice from underneath Hilda's jumper.

"Shush," Hilda hissed. "Mum mustn't know you're here. Just be quiet until we're safe in the bedroom, OK?"

Mum came out into the corridor. She was wearing blue overalls and had splashes of white paint on her hair and cheeks.

"Darling, I'm glad you're back! How was your day?"

"Overall, pretty traumatic," said Hilda. "Miss Hallgrim wants us to prepare a Wonderful Trolberg exhibition. Can you believe that? What will next week's homework be? Wonderful diseases?

Wonderful shipwrecks?"

"You poor thing," said Mum. "I'm sorry you're having a hard time."

Before Hilda could stop her, Mum hurried forward and gathered her up into a tight hug.

"Hey! You're smothering me!" croaked the raven.

"What?" Mum sounded confused.

"You're mothering me ... er ... really well," said Hilda.

"I do my best," chuckled Mum, releasing Hilda from the hug.

Hilda hurried along the corridor towards her bedroom.

"Shoes!" called Mum. Hilda went back, took her shoes off and placed them neatly beside the front door.

"Are we safe in the bedroom yet?" piped a voice.

Mum frowned. "What did you just say?"

Hilda could feel herself blushing. "I said, have you painted my bedroom yet?"

Mum frowned. "One thing at a time, Hilda.

I've only just started on the living room."

"Sure. No rush." Hilda turned and ran to her bedroom.

Hilda's bedroom in Trolberg was very bare. Most of her toys and games had been crushed when Jørgen the Ancient Giant had trodden on their old home. The most important things had survived, though, such as her deer fox friend, Twig, a little white bundle of courage and cuteness who often accompanied Hilda on her adventures.

Twig jumped down off Hilda's bed and padded towards her, sniffing the air and growling softly. He could sense that Hilda was not alone.

Hilda took the injured bird from underneath her jumper and placed it on a folded blanket in the corner of the room. "Twig, meet Raven," she said. "He was attacked by some awful children and now he can't fly."

Twig approached Raven. They eyed each other with suspicion.

"There's one more person you should meet,"

said Hilda. "Alfur, are you here?"

"Coo-ee!" called Alfur. "Nice to meet you,
Mr Raven. Would you mind if I interviewed you
for one of my 'Letter from Trolberg' elf reports?
How does it feel to be attacked by awful children?"

Raven sat bolt upright and his beak twitched
in alarm. "Where's that voice coming from?"
he stammered.

"Alfur is sitting on my desk," said Hilda.
"Elves are tiny – and also invisible until you sign
a bunch of forms."

"Okaaay." The raven looked confused.
"A blue-haired girl, a deer fox and an invisible elf.
Fair enough. I've seen stranger things. Or have I?
I'm not sure."

Alfur grabbed his notebook and jumped from
desk to chair and from chair to carpet. "What's
your name, Mr Raven?" he asked.

"Uh … I don't know."

"How old are you?"

"Pass."

"How do you spend your time here in the city?"

"I have absolutely no idea." The raven looked up at Hilda with wide, frightened eyes. "Oh, no! I don't remember anything! I've completely lost my memory, um ... Matilda!"

The following morning the raven still had no idea who he was or where he came from. He just lay there in his corner staring gloomily at the wall.

"You need to rest," Hilda told him. "Stay in your box today and get as much sleep as possible. If you need anything, ask Alfur."

"Hey!" Alfur clambered up into Hilda's ear. "Much as I'd love to spend the day playing elf-servant to your brainless friend, you did promise that I could come to school with you today. I'm researching an elf report about Trolberg schools, remember?"

"Oh," said Hilda. "All right, you can come with me. Just make sure you keep quiet in class."

The first two lessons of the day were science and maths. Alfur sat on Hilda's desk, writing fast in his tiny notebook. He seemed to love listening to Miss Hallgrim droning on, and he was making almost as many notes as Frida.

As soon as Miss Hallgrim turned her back on the class to write a sum on the blackboard, Hilda felt a tap on her shoulder.

"*Psst.* How's the bird?"

Hilda turned and saw Trevor sitting at the desk behind her.

"Leave me alone," she whispered. "You're a vile, vindictive varmint."

"I don't know those words," whispered Trevor, "but I'm sorry about yesterday, truly I am."

Hilda blinked. She hadn't expected that. "I'm as sorry as sorry can be," whispered Trevor. "By the way, can I borrow the bird for a bit?"

"No."

"Just for a few days. I want it for my Wonderful Trolberg exhibit."

"No."

"I'll be the envy of the whole class."

"No."

"You can't pretend the bird didn't speak, Hilda. I heard it."

"You imagined it."

Trevor slapped his desk in annoyance, then reached forward and pulled Hilda's hair.

"OW!" cried Hilda.

Miss Hallgrim whirled round to face the class. "Who was that?" she demanded.

"OW!" shrieked Trevor.

Miss Hallgrim glared at him.

"HEY!" shouted Trevor. "Someone poked me in the eye, Miss. EEK! They just did it again."

Miss Hallgrim's mouth was a thin, hard line. "No one is poking you in the eye, Trevor."

Trevor stood up and started contorting his face into all sorts of crazy expressions. He gaped. He grinned. He goggled and gurned.

"Trevor!" Miss Hallgrim strode forward. "Stop playing the fool!"

Only Hilda could see what was really going on. Invisible to everyone but her, Alfur was standing on Trevor's upper lip, pulling Trevor's cheeks into sillier and sillier positions.

"Go and stand in the corridor till lunchtime, Trevor," Miss Hallgrim said. "I shall write to your parents about this disgraceful behaviour."

As Trevor hurried out of the classroom, Hilda gave Alfur a cheerful thumbs up. Perhaps school could be fun, after all.

After school, Trevor confronted Hilda in the playground. "I don't know how you did it," he said, "but I know it was you."

"What was?"

"My face going all witchety-twitchety."

Trevor scowled at the memory. "And I still want that raven for my exhibit, so you'd better bring it to me tomorrow or there'll be trouble."

Hilda smiled at her enemy. It had been a happy day and she wasn't going to let anyone spoil it now. "You don't know me, Trevor," she said. "I've outwitted water spirits. I've calmed weather spirits. I've looped the loop on the back of a woff. Do you think I'm scared of any trouble you can give me?" With that, she turned and strolled off through the playground, Trevor staring after her open-mouthed.

Frida and David were waiting for her at the gate. "Come on!" Frida called. "Let's go get those bonus points."

David was looking much less confident. "Yes," he muttered. "Let's go and get devoured by hungry trolls."

"It's fine," Hilda reassured him. "Trolls don't hunt during the day."

The three children walked along together with the warm afternoon sun on their faces. At Lovelock Bridge, Frida stopped to pick some purple thistle.

"Boring," sighed Hilda, but Frida and David were not to be deterred. They went on to collect crabgrass by the church and dandelions from behind the grocer's shop.

At last they arrived at the ancient city wall in the shadow of Mount Hár. The wall was at least three metres high and was covered in ivy and huldermoss. David had been right about the brickwork being in a bad state of repair. From where she was standing, Hilda could see cracks and holes everywhere.

"Synchronize watches," said Frida.

"I don't have a watch," said Hilda. "When I want to know what time it is, I just glance at the position of the sun."

"Oh." Frida looked down at the clipboard in her hand. "That might be a problem, because I've planned each stage of this mission down to the exact minute. Three thirty: synchronize watches.

Three thirty-one: start looking for the blue nettle. Three thirty-two: keep looking for— Hey! Come back! It's not three thirty-one yet!"

Hilda set off in the shadow of the city wall, keeping her eyes peeled for a telltale flash of blue and trying to resist scratching her ear. With Alfur on board she was never alone, but the ticklish feeling was hard to get used to.

"Hilda, wait!" Frida ran to catch up with her. "Hilda, I just heard a really strange sound."

Hilda stopped and listened. Sure enough, she did hear something: eerie murmurs floating on the wind.

"I know that sound," said Hilda. "Don't worry, Frida, it's just elves."

"It's not just elves," whispered Alfur.

"The house I used to live in was surrounded by elf houses," said Hilda. "I've met more elves than you've had hot dinners, Frida. Hundreds of the blighters."

"It's not just elves," repeated Alfur.

"I love elves," said Hilda. "If there's any talking to do, Frida, leave it to me."

"IT'S NOT JUST ELVES!" Alfur yelled in her ear. "IT'S WILD ELVES, AND THAT'S COMPLETELY DIFFERENT."

Out from behind a clump of huldermoss filed a platoon of tiny warriors with warpaint on their faces and spears in their hands. They raised their weapons in perfect unison and pointed them at the girls. *Shink!*

A hairy elf stepped forward from the line.

He blew a horn and yelled one single terrifying word:

"ATTACK!"

5

Tiny spears whizzed through the air towards Hilda and Frida. Nuts and pebbles flew from hidden catapults. Sparrows with elf riders dive-bombed them from the top of the wall.

As Hilda and Frida turned to run, one unit of elves extended a tripwire, knocking them to the ground. Cavalry elves charged at them on rabbits, with long ropes trailing behind. The rabbits hopped back and forth around them, roping the children's arms and legs, and soon Hilda and Frida were trussed up so tight they could not move an inch.

Lying on her side, Hilda could see David further along the wall, and he was tied up too.

"What just happened?" wailed Frida. "Where are the elves? I can't see them."

"Elves are invisible," whispered Hilda. "I'll explain later."

The hairy elf with the horn stepped forward. "Greetings, intruders," he said. "My name is Bartel."

"Bartel Braga!" cried Alfur, jumping down from Hilda's ear. "Leader of the Lost Clan of the Northern Counties. I've heard lots about you."

Bartel beamed and stroked his beard. "All good, I trust."

"Not all of it," Alfur admitted. "I've heard you don't ever do paperwork."

At the mention of paperwork, a snort of anger rose from the wild elves, along with cries of "Burn all paper!" and "Down with forms!"

Bartel Braga approached Alfur and looked him up and down. "Who told you about us?"

he demanded.

"My grandmother," said Alfur. "When I was little, she used to recite an epic poem about the day you guys got exiled. Would you like to hear it?"

Bartel looked torn between fury and curiosity. "Go on," he said at last.

Alfur lowered his voice to a doom-laden whisper and began to chant.

"Long ago two ancient tribes,
Assembled on a plain.
Each clan sent forth eleven scribes,
To barter for terrain.

The Bragas meant to sell some land,
The Aldrics meant to buy it.
They did the paperwork by hand,
And then began to sign it."

At the mention of paperwork, the wild elves emitted a chorus of angry tuts and groans.

"Alfur, hold on a second," interrupted Hilda. "Is the subject of this epic poem *paperwork*?"

"Of course." Alfur looked surprised. "All our epic poems are about paperwork."

"You have a funny idea of what's epic."

"Relax," said Alfur. "The exciting bit is coming up. The elves are about to present the contract to be verified by the Elf Queen."

"Sounds amazing," sighed Hilda. "Go on, then, get on with it."

"They gave the contract to the Queen,
She studied every sheet.
Her face went red. 'What's this?' she said.
'The contract's incomplete!'

Chief Braga quaked before the Queen,
A crime had been committed!
A signature on page sixteen,
Had somehow been omitted.

'Be off with you!' the Elf Queen bayed.

'All Bragas will be EXILED!'

And that was the day she sent them away,

To live in the wilderness wild."

"That's insane!" exclaimed Hilda. "You're saying the Elf Queen sent the whole Braga clan into exile just because their chief forgot one signature?"

"Exactly," said Bartel Braga. "Now you understand why we detest paperwork. And also, why we detest Aldrics."

"I'm sure you don't really detest Aldrics," said Hilda. "Alfur here is an Aldric, and it's impossible to detest him. Just look at his little face."

Shink. The Bragas raised their spears in unison, the sharp ends all pointing at Alfur.

"Thanks, Hilda," Alfur muttered.

"Is this true, elf?" Bartel Braga demanded. "Are you an Aldric?"

Alfur trembled and stammered. "Yes, all right,

I am an Aldric, but I don't have anything against Bragas. I'm sure we can discuss this situation in a friendly manner—"

Before he could say another word, the cavalry elves charged at Alfur on rabbits, with fine threads trailing behind them. The rabbits hopped to and fro in a criss-crossing motion, binding Alfur's arms and legs until he was trussed up just as tightly as the three human children.

The Bragas glared at their captives and the captives glared back at them.

"What now?" said Hilda.

"Now," said Bartel Braga, "you fight."

"Who with?"

"With Ancient Agnes here. She will challenge you to battle one by one."

A wild-haired elf woman stepped forward out of line and snapped her spear across her knee.

"That's not fair!" cried Hilda. "David and Frida can't even SEE Agnes!"

"She can't see so well herself," said Bartel

Braga. "She's ninety-two, you know."

"But we're tied up!"

"Just do your best."

Someone brought Ancient Agnes a new spear, which she thrust into the air with a ferocious war cry. "Who's first?" she shrieked. "Who will fight me?"

"Wait a second," said Hilda. "So far as I can see, the Aldric elves are not the problem here, and neither are you Bragas. The problem is the incomplete contract! Do you still have it, Bartel?"

"Of course. One of the elders keeps it safe. And before you ask, the answer is no. We're not signing page sixteen or anything else for that matter. We have sworn off paperwork until the End of Time."

"Fair enough," said Hilda. "But if we simply destroy the contract, everything can go back to how it was before."

The chieftain stared at Hilda and then began to laugh. He slapped his thigh and wiped his eyes and chuckled fit to burst. Behind him, Ancient Agnes and the other troops were laughing their heads off

and the other troops were laughing their heads off too. Even Alfur was shaking with mirth as much as his bindings allowed him to.

"Who's going to tell her?" Bartel sniggered.

"Tell me what?" retorted Hilda.

"An elf contract can't be destroyed! Even if you tear it up into a thousand pieces and burn each shred and stomp on the ashes in hobnailed boots and scatter them in the river, *the contract itself remains valid*. I'm telling you now, Blue-Haired Girl, there's only one thing under heaven that can cancel an elf contract, and that is the flame from the nostrils of a lindworm!"

Hilda grinned. "I knew there must be something," she said. "Give us till sunset, Bartel, and I promise you we'll find a lindworm and get that contract cancelled."

Hilda and Frida walked back towards Trolberg
with the Bragas' tiny contract in her adventuring
satchel. Alfur rode in Hilda's ear and Frida
followed behind. Neither of the girls had said
a word since they had left the Lost Clan, but Alfur
was doing enough talking for all three of them.

"I'm amazed they let us go," the elf was saying.
"We wouldn't have stood a chance against that
Ancient Agnes – a lean, mean fighting machine
if ever I saw one. It's a pity Bartel insisted
on keeping David as a hostage, but you win some,
you lose some, right? I can't wait to get home and

start writing my report about the Lost Clan of the Northern Counties."

"We're not going home," Hilda said. "We're going to find a lindworm."

Alfur giggled nervously. "You misunderstand," he said. "All elf contracts have that 'flames from the nose of a lindworm' clause, but it's basically like saying 'when cows fly'. It's just a clever way of talking about something that will never ever ever ever ever *ever* happen."

Hilda took Alfur out of her ear and placed him on the palm of her hand. "Alfur, listen to me. I got David into this mess and I'm going to get him out of it. So tell me right now: where do we find a lindworm?"

"You don't," said Alfur. "Read my lips: lindworms are incredibly rare. Some people say that lindworms don't even exist."

"Trolberg library!" cried Hilda.

"You definitely won't find one there."

Hilda didn't bother replying. She was off and

running, squelching through mud and leaping over rocks. She needed information, fast.

Hilda arrived at the library and approached the information desk. The librarian looked about the same age as Hilda's mum, only much more stylish. The tips of her glossy black hair were dyed bright green.

"Here you go," said the librarian, passing her a book.

Hilda looked down and wiped a thick layer of dust off the cover. "*A Guide to the Serpents and Worms of Trolberg*," she read. "Wait, how on earth did you know—"

But when Hilda looked up, the librarian had disappeared. She was standing in the history section, helping another customer.

Hilda sat down at a desk. Frida arrived and plonked herself down next to her, red-faced and panting. "Here goes," said Hilda, flicking through the pages. Libbyworm... Lickyworm... Lidlworm... Lilyliver... Limboworm... Aha, here we are! *Lindworm!*"

"What does it say?" panted Frida.

"It says a lindworm is an antisocial, flammiferous carnivore. What does *flammiferous* mean?"

"Produces flame."

"I see." Hilda turned back to the book. "All the lindworms fled Trolberg when it was being built, and now only one lindworm lair remains in the entire province."

"Look," said Frida, pointing. "There's a tiny footnote. It says the location of the lair can be found in *Habitats and Hideouts, Volume*

Twenty-seven, Section Three."

Another dusty book landed on the desk in front of the girls, making them cough and splutter.

"You're welcome," said the librarian, and then, with a swish of her black satin cape, she disappeared.

Hilda looked at the cover of the book. "*Habitats and Hideouts, Volume Twenty-seven*," she read. "Wow. That lady is so going to win Librarian of the Year."

Frida seized the book, flicked to Section Three and pointed to a tiny island in the middle of the fjord. "There it is," she said. "Cauldron Island. Hey, where are you going? Aren't you going to put the books back?"

"No time for that!" Hilda called over her shoulder. "The Bragas said we had to be back before sunset, remember? And who knows what Ancient Agnes will do if we're late!"

Hilda and Frida had to run through Hilda's neighbourhood on their way to the harbour, and Hilda realised that they had picked up an extra companion. Her trusty deer fox, Twig, was bounding along at her heels, ready for adventure.

However, when they got to the harbour, they were in for a big disappointment. The sailors at Trolberg harbour refused to take them to Cauldron Island. *Too far*, they said. *Too dangerous*, they said. *That island is cursed*, they said.

"I'll take you," piped up a one-eyed fisherman, "so long as you give me the deer fox in return."

"No way." Hilda scooped Twig into her arms. "Not in a million years."

The fisherman chuckled into his beard and went back to mending his nets. Hilda stamped her foot in frustration.

"I have an idea," whispered Alfur in her ear.

"What is it?"

"You see that conch shell over there? Try giving it a blow."

Hilda reached down and picked up the conch shell, which had beautiful orange and white stripes along its twisted spire.

"Break the tip off the spire," said Alfur,
"then blow into the hole as hard as you can."

Hilda did as she was told. When she blew into
the conch, a clear, high trumpet call sounded over
the waves.

"What are you playing at?" snapped Frida.
"While you're tootling on that shilly she-sell,
I mean silly she-shell, I mean silly seashell, poor
David is lying tied up in the middle of— WOAH!
WHAT IS THAT THING?"

With a thunderous WHOOSH, a tall column
of water rose up in front of them and two watery
eyes blinked open.

"Sorry," said the water spirit. "I thought I heard
a female water spirit over here, and quite a tuneful
one at that. Well, my mistake."

"That was us," said Hilda. "We were hoping
you could give us a ride to Cauldron Island."

"No problem," said the water spirit. "Over the
water or under it?"

"Over, please," said Hilda.

A watery staircase appeared. Hilda, Frida and Twig walked up it and perched on the spirit's head.

"Where do we hold on?" stammered Frida.

"We don't." Hilda grinned. "Just pretend you're balancing on a surfboard."

Frida stuck her arms out and squeezed her eyes tight shut.

As the water spirit zoomed across the bay, a small rocky island appeared on the horizon. The spirit headed for the island and deposited its passengers on a stony beach.

"My bum's all wet," said Frida. "And my school bag."

Hilda curtseyed to the water spirit. "What she means to say is: thank you, kind spirit. Any chance you could wait here for our return journey?"

"You won't need one," said the spirit cheerfully. "Nobody who comes here ever needs a return journey, if you get my drift."

"Oh." Hilda swallowed hard. "OK."

The girls trudged up the beach. Alfur rode in Hilda's ear and Twig ran ahead.

"According to the book," said Frida, "the signs of a lindworm lair include disturbed leaves, overturned earth and—"

"Dark smoke?" said Hilda. She pointed to the centre of the island, where plumes of purple smoke curled high into the air.

"Well spotted," said Frida. "We'd better hurry, though. We've only got an hour or so before sunset."

At the top of the beach the stones got bigger and bigger. Soon the two girls were clambering over enormous rocks and jumping from one to the next, holding hands for the most difficult bits. One rock was so huge that Hilda had to stand on Frida's shoulders and then pull her up after.

Eventually, they found themselves descending into a hidden valley. They walked over shrinking nila grass, through lilac bush and wild sage, then on past giant rofflewort and gold and silver saxifrage.

"This place is incredible," whispered Frida.

"It's like a proper garden."

Twig was gambolling on ahead, then suddenly stopped on the edge of a clearing. Hackles rose on the back of his neck. This must be the lindworm's lair.

Hilda took a deep breath. "For David," she whispered.

"For David," echoed Frida.

They stepped forward into the clearing. Asleep in the middle was a colossal beast that looked half-dragon, half-serpent. Its large head and snout rested on a long, coiled body, covered in overlapping green and yellow scales.

"Woah," Frida whispered. "THAT'S a lindworm?"

"Of course," whispered Hilda. "What were you expecting?"

"A worm," squeaked Frida.

Purple smoke trailed from the dragon's nostrils and with every snore it emitted a little burst of flame.

"This is perfect," said Hilda. "We don't even

have to wake it up. We can just hold the contract in front of its nose and - *poof* - problem solved."

Hilda delved in her school bag and took out the contract. Sneaking towards the sleeping serpent with trembling hands, Hilda placed the tiny stack of papers underneath its two enormous nostrils.

The lindworm inhaled.

She stepped back and waited for the flame.

And waited.

And waited.

"Breathe out," whispered Hilda. "Come on. Breathe out."

The dragon twitched its scaly ears.

"Oh," said Hilda.

The dragon shifted on its haunches.

"Oh dear," said Hilda.

The dragon's massive eyelids fluttered open.

"RUN!" yelled Hilda.

7

Hilda snatched up the contract and darted off, but the lindworm slapped its tail down in front of her, blocking her way. It had huge plates of camouflaged armour all down its back.

"Who are you?" growled the lindworm, its pupils narrowing to furious slits. "And why were you sneaking up on me in my sleep?"

"Me?" said Hilda. "Sneaking up on you? All right, yes, I suppose you could call it sneaking up on you. Let me explain—"

But the lindworm had already spied the contract in her hand. "Oh, I see. Another elf trying to get out of a contract. What is it this time?

"A short-term lease? A non-disclosure agreement? I moved out here to get a little privacy, but you people still find a way to bother me, don't you? *Ooh, please, kind lindworm, give us a puff of fire. Pretty please, Lindy-loo, just one puff and we'll be on our way.* WELL, I'M TIRED OF IT, DO YOU HEAR ME? I'M FED UP TO THE HYDROGEN GLANDS! WHY SHOULD I GIVE AWAY MY PRECIOUS TALENTS FOR FREE? I DEVOURED THOSE OTHERS AND I'LL DEVOUR YOU AS WELL!"

The lindworm reared up and sucked in a huge mouthful of air. At that exact moment Twig leaped over its tail and darted in front of its snout, barking and growling. Tongues of fire belched from the dragon's nostrils. The deer fox dodged the first flame but the second flame singed the tip of his fluffy white tail.

Twig had succeeded in distracting the lindworm just long enough for Hilda to scramble up that rough scaly tail and down the other side to where Frida stood wide-eyed and quivering.

"Run!" cried Hilda, grabbing Frida's hand.

Together they dashed off into the trees and the lindworm slithered after them, pounding the earth with its strong forelegs. Its overlapping scales made a soft scraping sound as they slid over each other.

Hilda and Frida had no idea where they were going, and it was not long before they reached a complete dead end – a wall of rock on the northern side of the lindworm's garden.

They were trapped.

As the lindworm cranked open its jaw and flexed its hydrogen glands, Hilda stepped forward with a huge smile on her face. "I love what you've done with the place!" she yelled.

The dragon hesitated. "Eh?"

"Your garden!" yelled Hilda. "I love it. Green fingers, that's what you've got."

The lindworm glanced uncertainly at its scaly claws.

"I see you've planted tufts of aster in amongst the goldenrod," continued Hilda. "The purple and the yellow go together beautifully. You're a genius!"

The lindworm simpered. "I do love gardening," it said. "Younger flashier dragons prefer gold coins and silver goblets, but plants are the real treasures of the earth, don't you think?"

"I do." Hilda nodded hard. "I agree with you one hundred per cent."

"I thought you might. Anyway, I can't stand here chatting all day. It's time to burn you to a crisp."

Hilda was out of ideas. She closed her eyes and hoped that death would come quickly.

"Wait!" Frida stepped forward, shoulder to shoulder with Hilda. "Don't burn us up. It would be a shame to frazzle all the lovely plant cuttings in my bag."

The lindworm eyed Frida's school bag. "Plant cuttings?"

"*Exciting* plant cuttings," said Frida, opening her bag and taking out the plants.

"*Exciting* might be an exaggeration,"

muttered Hilda.

The lindworm's eyes narrowed. "Crabgrass? Purple thistle? Dandelions? WOWEE! I've been trying to get my hands on some good city flowers for years now, but I'm too shy to visit Trolberg. Would you let me keep these beautiful cuttings? I would happily burn your contract in return."

"And not harm us?" said Frida.

The lindworm rolled its eyes. "Ugh, if you insist."

The water spirit was amazed to see its passengers emerge unscathed from the lindworm's lair.

"You're sure you met the creature?" it asked.

"Yes," said Hilda.

"And you're still alive?"

Hilda pinched herself. "Apparently," she said.

Frida glared at the water spirit. "Cut the small talk," she said. "We need to get back to the Lost Clan of the Northern Counties before sunset or our friend David will have to fight Ancient Agnes."

"First World problems," muttered the spirit.

"Come on then, hop on."

The sky was a blaze of crimson and orange, and the sun was already kissing the horizon. Hilda and Frida zoomed back across the fjord, jumped onto the dock of the bay and sprinted through the city all the way to the outer wall.

"Bartel!" Hilda yelled. "Bartel, we're back!"

Warrior elves emerged from the huldermoss, blocking the way. They raised their weapons. *Shink!*

"Howdy-doodie!" cried a voice high above them. Hilda looked up and saw Bartel Braga standing on top of the wall. As she watched, he wrapped a vine around his waist and leaped off, whooping with glee as he swooped towards the ground.

"Show-off," whispered Hilda.

Bartel landed on his feet, untied the vine and bowed. "You can clap if you like," he said.

Alfur jumped down onto Hilda's shoulder, beaming from ear-to-ear and clapping his handless arms nineteen to the dozen. "Bravo!" he cried. "*Encore!*"

"Where's David?" asked Hilda.

"All in good time," said Bartel. "First, I want to see what you've got for me."

Frida arrived beside Hilda, puffing and panting. She opened up her school bag and tipped its contents onto the ground. The wild elves pressed forward to look. A tiny pile of ash glowed green and gold in the gathering gloom.

"That glow," breathed Bartel. "Lindworm flame!"

Alfur beamed. "Your exile is over," he said, "and so is your quarrel with the Aldrics."

Bartel jumped for joy and high-fived Alfur. "Terrific!" he cried. "Agnes, go and tell Rope Unit Three to untie our dim-witted hostage."

A minute or two later, David appeared, pale but unharmed. Frida took a moment to brush the twigs and leaves from his clothes, as well as a whole colony of bugs from his hair.

Alfur put his arm around his new friend Bartel. "How are you feeling?" he said. "You do realise you're free to go back to the valley now and can live like normal elves?"

"Live like normal elves?" Bartel echoed, the smile fading from his face. "Live in houses, you mean?"

"Yes."

"With biros and bank accounts?"

"Indeed."

"House cats? Hoovers? Hairbrushes?"

"And lots of other stuff, yes."

"Ugh." Bartel shuddered. "No offence, Alfur, but I think we might stay in the wild after all."

8

Hilda lay on her bed that evening, thinking about how strange human children could be. She had gone to a lot of trouble to rescue David but he had gone straight home without a word, not even a simple "thank you".

It was doubly odd because in fact the mission had turned out to be a huge success. Each of them had taken a blue nettle cutting before leaving, and David had grabbed some cool-looking rocks too. He had every reason to be happy, so why on earth did he seem so cross?

Frida was no better. On the way home, when Hilda complimented her for her quick thinking in the lindworm's lair, Frida just grunted in response. No smile, no laughter, no sharing of feelings. Just a grunt, then silence.

Hilda could not understand why Mum was so keen for her to have human friends. Magical friends were better in every way. Magical friends were friends you could trust.

Hilda looked fondly at her magical room-mates. Twig was curled up snoring at the foot of her bed. Alfur sat at the desk, writing a 'Letter from Trolberg' about the day's adventures. As for the talking raven, he lay on his blanket with his wings stretched out, humming tunelessly.

"Hey, Mr Raven," said Hilda. "Do you remember your name yet?"

"No."

"Do you remember *anything* about yourself?"

"No." The raven rolled his eyes. "I don't even remember how to fly. My wings are fine, but I can't remember how to use them. So humiliating!"

"Oh dear." Hilda giggled. "You really need to take a memory pill, don't you?"

As soon as the words were out of her mouth, Hilda had an idea. She looked at the raven, then at her school bag by the door, then back at the raven. She remembered what she had told Frida: *Blue nettle is not like green nettles... it's supposed to be good for your brain.*

Hilda ran to fetch her blue nettle cutting. "Here, eat this," she said, putting it down in front of the raven.

The raven pecked the corner of a leaf and cocked his head on one side.

"Well?" said Hilda. "Do you remember anything?"

"Yes!" cried the raven. "I'm important!"

Hilda frowned. "Everyone thinks that about themselves."

The raven ate another leaf, and then another. Before long, he had gobbled the whole thing.

"That was my Wonderful Trolberg exhibit,"

said Hilda.

"Tastiest exhibit I've ever eaten," said the raven. "Or is it? I'm not sure."

Tummy bulging, the raven lay back on his blanket and closed his eyes as if to go to sleep. All of a sudden, a violent shiver passed through his body and he sat bolt upright.

"I remember!" the raven cried. "I remember a gigantic statue!"

"Well done!" said Hilda. "What did it look like?"

"A bald man with a beard and a cape! I landed on the statue, and I looked down at the people below."

"Brilliant!" cried Hilda. "And what were the people doing?"

"They were looking up at me!"

"And what happened next?"

"Something amazing!" cried the raven.

"But I can't remember what. Good night ... Gilda."

The next day at school, Hilda's class made decorations for the school float. They made thousands of paper flowers, hundreds of paper birds and one enormous papier-mâché model of Edmund Ahlberg, founder of their school.

Hilda watched with growing confusion as the papier-mâché model took shape. When the bell rang for morning break, she went over to Miss Hallgrim and tugged on her sleeve.

"Excuse me, Miss," she said. "Why is there a sleeping troll at Edmund Ahlberg's feet?"

"It's not sleeping," said Miss Hallgrim. "It's dead."

"Dead?" cried Hilda.

"Of course," said Miss Hallgrim. "Didn't you listen to a SINGLE WORD of our history lesson last week? Edmund Ahlberg was the greatest trollslayer our city has EVER seen."

Hilda stared at her teacher. "But... but... that's terrible!" she cried. "Why are we celebrating such a cruel, wicked man? Why are you making us parade around the city with a papier-mâché model of a murderer? Who gave him the right to kill poor, defenceless trolls?"

Miss Hallgrim pursed her lips. "Don't be difficult, Hilda," she said. "Edmund Ahlberg was a GREAT man and this school would NOT EXIST without him. And whilst I am on the subject of BEING DIFFICULT, I am sorry to tell you, Hilda, that I have received complaints about your behaviour OUTSIDE SCHOOL."

"Outside school?"

"Near the city wall, to be precise."
Miss Hallgrim fixed Hilda with a glittering eye.

"Oh," said Hilda. "I see."

"In view of this behaviour, Frida and David's parents have asked me to adjust the Wonderful Trolberg working groups. Frida and David will go ahead with their exhibit of Trolberg PLANTS, and you, Hilda, will prepare an entirely different exhibit ON YOUR OWN."

Hilda felt sad all afternoon. Frida and David were both perfectly polite whenever she spoke to them, but not what you would call friendly. David in particular kept casting nervous glances in her direction, as if at any moment she might click her fingers to summon a horde of rabbit-riding warrior elves.

Trevor, on the other hand, was being weirdly chummy. *"How's the bird, Hilda?"* he kept saying. *"How's the bird? By the way, Hilda, I think you're going to love my Wonderful Trolberg exhibit. I can't wait for you to see it!"*

Hilda had noticed that her most traumatic days at school were also the days that seemed to last the longest. This one must have lasted a hundred years already. But the home time bell did finally ring, along with all the other bells in the city.

Hilda hoisted her school bag onto her shoulder and fled out of the classroom, out of the building and out of the gate. Past the train station and the Nils Pills Pharmacy. Across the river at the Bronstad Lane footbridge. Past the Scout Hall, past the grocer's, past a zillion horrible houses and all the way back home.

With a heavy heart, Hilda dragged herself up the three flights of stairs and let herself into the flat. Mum was right there in the hallway, spreading paint in long white arcs.

"Ugh," said Hilda.

"Good afternoon to you too," said Mum. "Do I get a hug?"

Hilda kicked off her shoes. "Our home used to smell of ginger and nutmeg and caraway seeds," she muttered. "Now it just smells of paint."

"Not for long," said Mum. "Five or six more days and the whole flat will be as clean and white as edelweiss."

"I don't like edelweiss."

"Tough." Mum reached out with the paintbrush and dabbed a spot of white paint right on the end of Hilda's nose.

Normally Hilda would have shrieked with laughter and leaped to wreak revenge, but she just stood there in the hallway with the blob of paint on the end of her nose, feeling very small and unhappy.

"Hilda, you're crying!" said Mum, pulling her into a tight hug. "Whatever is the matter?"

Hilda pressed her face into Mum's shoulder and her words came out in one great long rush. "I thought I had two friends at school and we went adventuring together but it was a teeny bit traumatic so now they're scared of me and their parents won't let me work with them and I have to do my own exhibit about Wonderful Trolberg but that's impossible because there's nothing wonderful about Trolberg and all I want is to go back to our cabin in the wilderness!"

Mum carried on hugging her and said nothing for a long time. "Hot chocolate?" she said at last.

Hilda nodded and forced a smile. Ten minutes later, mother and daughter sat down on the living-room sofa with mugs of rich, steaming chocolate in their hands.

"To be perfectly honest," said Mum, "I don't think much of your friends' exhibit. That bird is probably riddled with disease."

Hilda stared at her. "What bird?"

"The raven. David came to pick it up after you left for school this morning. I told him there were no birds in this house, and he said you were probably keeping it in your bedroom, and hey presto, there it was! I'm not cross with you, Hilda, but I do wish you would ask me before bringing straggle-feathered old— Hey, where are you going?"

Hilda had slammed her mug down on the table and charged out of the room, along the corridor and into her bedroom. Twig was there at the foot of her bed, but the blanket box in the corner was empty.

"What did he look like?" Hilda cried, rushing back into the living room.

"Beady eyes, dirty black feathers—"

"Not the bird, the boy!" Hilda stamped her foot. "The boy who called himself David. What did he look like?"

"Black hair, I think," said Mum. "Bright red cheeks. Orange hat with ear flaps."

"That's not David," Hilda wailed. "That's Trevor!"

"Is he another of your friends?"

"No, he's not, he's the meanest boy in the whole school."

Mum looked confused. "If he's not your friend, how did he know where you lived?"

"We're new in town," said Hilda, "and also, I'VE GOT BLUE HAIR."

"That's true." Mum smiled. "We don't exactly

blend in, do we? It wouldn't take anyone long to find out our address."

Hilda could not believe her mum was smiling at a moment like this. She should be throwing herself at Hilda's feet, begging for forgiveness, but instead she was just sitting there on the sofa, slurping hot chocolate and smiling her head off.

Hilda ran back to her bedroom and threw herself down on the bed, furious at Mum for giving the raven to Trevor and furious with herself for not hiding it properly in the first place. Poor Raven! Tomorrow he would be dragged along to the Wonderful Trolberg exhibition, where he would no doubt be poked and prodded and forced to talk.

"Alfur, are you there?" Hilda whispered, wiping away her tears.

"Right here." Alfur poked his head out from behind the bedside lamp. "How can I be of service?"

"You can come with me to the exhibition at school tomorrow," said Hilda.

CHAPTER NINE

"Raven's been kidnapped."

"Oh no!" said Alfur.

"And we're going to rescue him."

"Oh yes!" said Alfur.

"Or die trying."

"Oh dear," said Alfur.

10

The day of the Great Parade dawned bright and clear. On this special day Hilda did not have to be in school until the Wonderful Trolberg exhibition in the afternoon, so she lay in bed as long as possible, listening to the radio. The weather forecast was on, and Victoria van Gale was predicting a cold, dry day with a gentle snowfall at seven forty-one in the evening.

"Seven forty-one," Alfur chuckled. "Victoria van Gale is very precise, isn't she?"

Hilda spent the morning reading and playing Dragon Panic with her mum. But she found it hard to concentrate. She kept thinking of the poor raven, wondering where he was and hoping Trevor was not hurting him.

It was a relief when three o'clock came round. Hilda grabbed her school bag, said goodbye to Mum and left for school with Alfur in her ear.

The first thing Hilda saw when she arrived at school was the Trollslayer float. It stood in the middle of the playground, overflowing with paper birds and flowers in every colour of the rainbow. In the middle of it all stood Edmund Ahlberg, sword in his hand, a lifeless troll at his feet and a sneer of triumph on his ugly papier-mâché face.

Inside the classroom the desks had been arranged in one long line around three sides of the walls, ready to display the children's exhibits. Streamers and paper chains hung from the ceiling. An enormous banner across the chalkboard read:

'WONDERFUL TROLBERG!'

Frida and David were already there, working on their flower arrangement, an elegant pyramid of rocks. Moss and crabgrass poked out between the stones and the hard-won posy of blue nettle stood proud on top. Right now, David was planting one last clump of moss into a gap at the bottom of the pyramid. As soon as he saw Hilda, his hand jerked in fright and the whole pile came clattering down on top of him.

Frida clicked her tongue in irritation. "David, you're so clumsy!" she said.

"Sorry," he muttered, crawling under the table to retrieve his rocks.

"Excuse me, you two," said Hilda stiffly. "Have you seen Trevor?"

"No," said Frida. "Why?"

"No reason. Please tell me if you see him."

Hilda went to the far end of the classroom and took from her school bag a small jar containing a dozen orange specks. She plonked the jar on a table and sat down next to it.

Frida eyed the jar suspiciously. "Is that your exhibit?" she asked.

"Yes," said Hilda.

"What is it?"

"Nittens," said Hilda.

Three weeks ago, for reasons beyond Hilda's control, a tiny brown elf cat had given birth in her hair. The kittens – or nittens, as Hilda called them – must have numbered at least one hundred, because whenever Hilda combed her hair these days a smattering of nittens would drop out. They looked cute under a magnifying glass, but in her hair they itched like crazy.

"I've never heard of nittens," said Frida. "They're certainly not a Trolberg thing."

"They are now," said Hilda.

David peered out from underneath his table. "Are n-n-nittens dangerous?" he stammered.

"Very," Hilda lied.

David yelped in fright and Alfur the elf started laughing fit to burst. "Naughty, naughty," he whispered to Hilda, and even though she still felt cross, she could not help smiling to herself.

The other children arrived in groups of three and started setting up their exhibits. There were feathers and acorns and leaves from the park. There were maplewood fiddles and dragonspruce harps. There were typewriters, teapots, cookie cutters, slingshots, coin collections, stamp collections, oil-burning lamp collections, hand bells, sleigh bells, night bells, day bells, chess sets, fishing nets, cameras and clocks.

Hilda stared at the amazing collection of objects. Perhaps 'Wonderful Trolberg' wasn't such an impossible idea after all.

Trevor was last to arrive. He swaggered into the classroom and hung a big sign on the front of his display table. There was no sign of the raven yet, but the words on the sign made Hilda's heart sink into her boots.

IT SPEAKS! IT SINGS! PREPARE TO BE AMAZED!

Hilda strode over to Trevor and grabbed his wrist. "Where is he?" she yelled. "Where is my raven?"

Trevor grinned. "It's not your raven, Hilda. It belongs to no one. It is happy and free, like all of Trolberg's creatures." Trevor sat down, put his feet on the table and started to hum tunelessly.

"You're so mean!" Hilda yelled. "You're the meanest person I've met in my whole life!"

She felt a tap on the shoulder and turned to see Miss Hallgrim looming over her.

"Hilda, that's QUITE enough," Miss Hallgrim said. "The parents will start arriving soon, and I will NOT let you put this class to SHAME, do you understand?"

"Yes, but—"

"I SAID, DO YOU UNDERSTAND!"

"Yes, Miss."

"Good. In that case, you will SIT down over there beside your jar of orange dirt and you will not move a muscle until the END of the exhibition."

11

At four o'clock, the parents arrived. They filed
into the classroom, grinning nervously, and sat
down in rows on plastic chairs that were much
too small for them. Miss Hallgrim stalked to the
front and waited for silence. The parents stopped
chattering and put their hands in their laps,
all except for Hilda's mum, who was waving at
Hilda like a loon. Hilda pretended not to notice.

"Welcome, one and all!" Miss Hallgrim
beamed. "Today is the MOST important day
of the Trolberg calendar, the day of the
GREAT PARADE. On behalf of class Four B,

I am DELIGHTED to introduce our exhibition on the theme of WONDERFUL TROLBERG."

The classroom door opened and in came Trevor again, this time carrying a cage. Imprisoned inside was a wide-eyed, frightened bird. When Raven saw Hilda, he raised a feeble wing to wave at her. Hilda clenched her fists as she watched Trevor carry Raven to his table and sit down.

Miss Hallgrim hated lateness and she shot Trevor a disapproving glance before continuing her speech. "Ladies and gentlemen, we BEGIN our exhibition with a short FILM about the history of our great city. Lights, Frida."

Frida switched off the lights and closed the blinds, plunging the classroom into darkness. A projector whirred into life. Animations of ancient Trolberg scrolled across the screen and a narrator began to speak.

"Trolberg was founded six hundred years ago. Brick by brick its city walls rose up between the mountains and the sea. But those were dangerous times.

The bloodthirsty trolls of Mount Halldór and Mount Hár were slow to understand that the land was no longer theirs. Our brave ancestors had to defend themselves against daily attacks..."

Hilda knew that her best chance to rescue Raven was under cover of darkness. She got down on all fours and started crawling between the rows of parents, heading for Trevor's table. She tried to listen out for raven squawks, but all she could hear was the history of Trolberg.

"One man did more than any other to trounce those troublesome trolls. The mighty Edmund Ahlberg killed so many trolls that people called him Trollslayer. To this day, the noble name of Ahlberg can be seen on buildings all over the city: the Edmund Ahlberg café, the Edmund Ahlberg barber shop, the Edmund Ahlberg primary school..."

Hilda had reached the display tables on the other side of the classroom. She reached up and felt along the surface. Her hands touched lamps and cameras and bells of every sort, but still no birdcage.

"Hurry up," Alfur whispered in her ear. "This film could end at any moment."

"As soon as the city walls were finished, the people of Trolberg built a statue of their god. They called him the raven god, because they believed he used ravens as messengers..."

As soon as she heard the word 'raven', Hilda looked up sharply. Pictured on the screen was a colossal stone statue of a bald man with a beard and a cape. A memory stirred at the back of Hilda's brain. Where had she heard about that statue recently?

While Hilda racked her brain, the film continued:

"One day a gigantic raven flew down out of the sky and perched on the shoulder of the raven god's statue. That year there was a great harvest. Everyone prospered. The people of Trolberg believed that the good harvest was caused by the Great Raven's visit, so they started an annual parade in its honour..."

"Are you thinking what I'm thinking?" Alfur

whispered in Hilda's ear. "Didn't our feathered friend say he thought he was important? And that he remembered perching on a baldy beardy statue in the middle of the city?"

"The parade continues to this day. Some call it the Great Parade. Others call it the Bird Parade. If the Great Raven appears in the sky on the day of the Bird Parade, the harvest that year will be good. If the Great Raven does not fly, then the harvest will fail and nobody will have enough to eat."

Hilda stared at the screen. Alfur was right. Her raven and the Great Raven were the *same bird*, a shape-shifter of some sort. And if he didn't fly at the Great Parade, the city would suffer greatly.

There was not a moment to lose. Trembling all over, Hilda stood up in the dark classroom full of parents and yelled at the top of her voice,

"Save the Great Raven!"

There was a short, shocked silence, and then a flash of light and a thunderous crash.

"Lights!" called Miss Hallgrim.

Frida opened the blinds and the afternoon sun streamed in through the windows. The parents gasped at the scene before them. The projector was on the floor, smashed to smithereens. Frida and David's rock pyramid lay scattered all over their table.

"Our lovely exhibit!" wailed Frida.

Miss Hallgrim glared at the wreckage. "What HAPPENED here?"

Frida stepped forward and pointed at a knobbly rock that lay among the remains of the projector. "It looks like someone threw one of our rocks at the projector, Miss."

All eyes turned to Hilda, who was standing next to the ruined pyramid. Even Mum was glaring at her.

"It wasn't me," said Hilda. "I know this looks bad, but honestly, it wasn't me."

"Really?" Miss Hallgrim pursed her lips. "Then WHY are you not sitting in your SEAT?"

Hilda pointed at the bird in Trevor's cage. "I was trying to rescue the Great Raven."

A gale of laughter filled the classroom.

Children and parents alike all hooted and howled and chuckled and jeered.

Miss Hallgrim's nostrils twitched in fury. "Hilda, I think you'll FIND that the Great Raven is quite a lot BIGGER than this one. Trevor's raven is what scientists call a NORMAL raven, an ORDINARY raven, a BOG-STANDARD COMMON-AS-MUCK RUN-OF-THE-MILL MEDIOCRE EVERYDAY RAVEN. Now go and sit down in your seat, before you embarrass your mother any further."

Hilda returned to her chair, her eyes pricking with tears.

Miss Hallgrim picked up the knobbly rock and examined it thoughtfully. "What a peculiar shape," she murmured. "I'd better lock it in my drawer before it takes someone's eye out."

12

As soon as the school caretaker finished sweeping up the broken projector, the exhibition began. Hilda sat slumped in her chair as a long line of parents shuffled past her table. Most of them did not even bother asking what was in her empty-looking jar. As for Miss Hallgrim, she kept staring coldly at Hilda, making sure she did not budge from her seat.

Hilda grabbed a piece of paper and a pencil, and scribbled a short note on it.

DEAR FRIDA,
I'M SORRY I PUT DAVID'S LIFE IN DANGER
AND I'M SORRY YOU NEARLY GOT FRAZZLED
BY THE LINDWORM. PLEASE FORGIVE ME.
I REALLY WANT US TO BE FRIENDS AGAIN.
LOTS OF LOVE
HILDA

"Hilda, what on earth got into you?" Mum had arrived at Hilda's table and she did not look happy.

"I didn't throw the rock," said Hilda. "And that raven over there *is* the Great Raven, I'm sure of it. When I fed him blue nettle the other night he remembered how important he is. He even remembered landing on the statue."

Mum reached out and felt Hilda's forehead. "I think you might be sick," she said.

"I'm not sick!" Hilda said. "Mum, you know how good I am with magical creatures! When will you start trusting me? That raven is the Great Raven, and we've got to make sure he flies at the parade."

Mum looked across the room. Trevor was leaning over the birdcage, wagging his finger as he scolded the raven. "*Come on,*" he urged. "*Talk, like you did last night. Say something. Anything!*"

Mum bit her lip and sighed. "OK, Hilda," she said at last. "What do you want me to do?"

Hilda grinned. "Thank you, Mum! You see that girl over there? Clipboard? Blue jumper? Yellow hair grips? I need you to give her this." She folded up the note for Frida and thrust it into Mum's hand.

As the line moved on, and Mum with it, Hilda's attention was caught by a strange rattling sound at the front of the classroom. It seemed to be coming from the drawer of the teacher's desk. It must be those jumping beans Miss Hallgrim had confiscated from Margie a few days ago.

Hilda looked around. No one else had noticed the commotion in Miss Hallgrim's desk drawer. They were all too engrossed in looking at the Wonderful Trolberg exhibits. But the more Hilda tried to ignore the sound, the more uneasy she felt. It was more of a knocking than a rattling, and it sounded louder than jumping beans. Also, was it her imagination, or was the whole desk shaking?

Hilda racked her brains. The only thing she had seen Miss Hallgrim put in that drawer was the odd-shaped rock that had smashed the projector. And the odd-shaped rock couldn't be making the knocking sound because no rock jumps around all by itself. Unless...

Unless it's a troll rock.

Get real, thought Hilda. The odd-shaped rock is much too small to be a troll rock. Unless...

Unless it's a baby troll rock.

No way, thought Hilda. You don't find baby troll rocks in Trolberg. Unless...

Unless a baby troll rock found its way into the city and someone picked it up.

Hilda gasped as she remembered her adventure with Frida and David at the city wall. Before leaving the Lost Clan they had each taken a blue nettle cutting, and David had grabbed some cool-looking rocks too.

It made sense. When the lights were turned off for the history film, the troll rock had come to life, jumped out of the pyramid and hurled itself at the projector. When the lights came back on, it had turned back into a rock. And now that it was locked in the darkness of Miss Hallgrim's desk drawer, the troll had come to life again and was trying to get out.

David had realised too. He hurried over to Hilda, his face as white as edelweiss.

"Hilda, you've got to help me," he stammered.

Hilda looked at him and raised an eyebrow. For months she had been practising her single eyebrow raise, and she was glad to have a chance to use it.

David blushed. "I'm sorry for being so unfriendly to you, Hilda."

"That's OK," smiled Hilda. "I'm sorry I pressured you to go after that blue nettle. Now, if you just take this invisible elf to Miss Hallgrim's desk drawer, he'll pick the lock for you, no problem."

"Troll rocks and invisible elves," groaned David. "It's like all my nightmares are coming true at once."

Hilda placed the elf in David's trouser pocket. He sneaked to the front of the class and Alfur picked the lock with his pointy arms. They were back within thirty seconds, David cupping the rock in his hands to shield it from passing parents.

"You did it!" Hilda whispered. "Well done, both of you. Now we just need to take it back where it belongs before sunset."

"I hate to be the one to tell you this," said Alfur, looking west, "but sunset is already here."

Alfur was right. The last ray of afternoon sun sparkled on the window, then faded and disappeared. The surface of the rock bubbled and bulged, and Hilda noticed two dark spots that looked like eyes. The troll uncurled, took one look at David and sank its teeth into his hand.

"Yarooo!" cried David, staggering sideways into Hilda's desk. The nitten jar smashed on the floor and Alfur fell off David's shoulder, landing in the hole of an old clay lamp.

The troll set off running along the display tables. It dashed across a dragonspruce harp – pling, plong, plung – and across a typewriter – tak-ta-ta-tak-tak! – then climbed into a slingshot and pulled itself backwards to stretch the elastic.

Wheeeeeeee! The tiny troll sailed through the air and disappeared into a ventilation grille in the wall of the classroom.

There was a knock on the door and
Mr Magnusson the head teacher poked his head
into the classroom. His eyes twinkled behind his
glasses and his enormous greying beard waggled
as he talked.

"Hello, hello, hello," he said. "Class Four B
seems to be having a merry time in here. Welcome,
parents. Good to see you all. Not long now until
we saddle up the school float and ride off to the
Bird Parade. I can already hear the pipes and the
drums and the ... oh dear." He tailed off, staring
out of the window in horror.

Hilda looked. An enormous grown-up troll had lumbered into the playground. It snuffled and snarled and sniffed the air with its long nose.

"Interesting," said Mr Magnusson. "Either that is a Bird Parade merrymaker wearing an excellent fancy dress costume, or ... OK, no, I think we can assume it's an actual troll. Dear me, I don't think this has ever happened before. Not since the days of Edmund Ahlberg, anyway. What do you think we should do, Miss Hallgrim?"

"SOUND THE TROLL ALARM!" shrieked Miss Hallgrim. "YOU HAVE ONE IN YOUR OFFICE!"

"Troll alarm." The head teacher twirled his moustache and nodded cheerfully. "That's a clever idea. You all hide under your desks and I'll sound the alarm. Toodle-pip!"

The head teacher gave the parents a nervous thumbs up, then disappeared, slamming the door behind him. Hilda heard the slap and scuff of his leather shoes as he legged it down the corridor towards his office.

"No! Wait!" cried Hilda. She ran from the classroom and dashed after him along the corridor. He was surprisingly speedy for a big man.

"Stop!" shouted Hilda.

"Can't chat now, poppet!" he replied, diving headlong into his office.

When Hilda burst in seconds later, Mr Magnusson was standing by the troll alarm on the wall. He had already flipped up the lid and was about to press the big red button inside.

"Please!" yelled Hilda. "Don't do that! We don't want a crisis!"

Mr Magnusson stared at her. "Sorry, poppet, but I'm afraid this is already a crisis."

"Don't!" repeated Hilda. "If you press that button, the whole city will panic and the troll police will kill the troll and David will go to jail for bringing a troll into the city."

The head teacher frowned. Still his finger hovered over the red button.

"Sir," Hilda pleaded, "I'm pretty sure the troll

out there is a mother who just who wants her baby back. I know where the baby is, sir. I can get it for her."

Mr Magnusson looked out of his window at the furious troll in the middle of the playground. Then he looked back at Hilda. "I'll give you one minute, poppet," he said at last. "Sixty seconds to find the baby troll and give it back to its mother. If you can't do it in that time, I shall have no choice but to press this button and summon the troll police."

"Fine," said Hilda. "And one more thing, sir."

"What's that?"

"My name's not poppet. It's Hilda."

Hilda rushed out of the office and back to the classroom. Everyone was huddled under the desks, trying to stay quiet. The only noise in the room came from inside the wall – the pitter-patter of tiny feet running to and fro along the air vent.

"Poor thing," murmured Hilda, pressing her ear to the wall. "It must be terrified."

"It's not the only one," muttered David,

who was cowering under a table to her left.

Hilda searched through the exhibition wreckage on the floor. She picked up an old coin and a fishing net.

"Hilda!" This time the voice was Mum's. "Come and take shelter!"

"Just a second," whispered Hilda. She crept to the ventilation grille and used the edge of the coin to undo the screws. Ever so gently she lifted the grille away from the air vent and placed it on the floor. Then she crouched down and listened as the pitter-patter of tiny feet zoomed along the wall towards the hole. Three ... two ... one ... NOW!

Hilda shoved the fishing net into the air vent.

As soon as she felt the pole jerk in her hand she tightened her grip and yanked it out again.

Everyone gasped. Caught at the bottom of the net was a furious troll baby with a long nose and a tiny tail. It smelled like stewed beets.

"David, open the window, quick!" said Hilda.

As it turned out, David did not need to open the window because just at that moment a ham-like troll fist smashed through the glass from the playground side. Mama Troll had caught the scent of her baby and she was coming for it, with or without permission.

Hilda put her hand in the net and pulled out the baby troll, holding it tight around its middle so it could not bite her. "Over here, Mama!" she shouted. "Here's your baby. He's fine."

Mama Troll snatched her baby, drew her hand back through the hole in the glass and lumbered off towards the school gates. Hilda watched as the troll paused for a moment next to the school float and glared up at the papier-mâché model of Edmund

'Trollslayer' Ahlberg. Mama Troll snarled, raised her fist high in the air, and then with one almighty wallop she crushed the model as flat as a pancake.

"Our lovely Edmund!" Miss Hallgrim wailed. "All that hard work!"

The troll galumphed towards the front gate and disappeared into the darkness with her baby in her arms.

Hilda felt a soft hand on her shoulder.

"You were amazing," said Mum. "I'm so proud of you!"

"Thanks, Mum," said Hilda.

They stood side by side, surveying the wreckage in the classroom. "I think the exhibition is over," said Mum, putting her hand over her mouth to hide a giggle. "Come on, darling, let's go. I know a high wall near the train station where we can perch to watch the Bird Parade go by."

"The Bird Parade!" cried Hilda. "I'd quite forgotten!"

All the other children and their parents were
coming out from underneath the desks and
brushing themselves down, but Trevor and the
raven were nowhere to be seen.

"Mum," said Hilda, "did you give Frida that
note I gave you?"

"Yes, of course."

"Thanks, Mum, I'll see you soon." Hilda kissed
her on the cheek and ran over to Frida. "Frida, are
you OK? Did you read my note?"

"Yes." Frida smiled. "It was a lovely note.

Thank you."

"So did you feed the blue nettle to the raven and set him free?"

"No. Not exactly." Frida looked at her feet. "I asked Trevor if I could do those things, but he said he would rather I didn't. He reminded me that there is a rule about not interfering with another student's exhibit. He advised me that I would probably lose marks if I tried any funny business."

"You ASKED him?!" Hilda could hardly believe her ears. "Frida, what's wrong with you? I'm trying to rescue the Great Raven and save the entire city from misery and hunger and the only thing you care about is following rules. Unbelievable! Where's Trevor now?"

"He left," said David, joining them. "He was really mad at the raven for refusing to talk. He said that since it wasn't in the mood for talking, maybe it was in the mood for swimming."

"Swimming?"

"That's what he said."

Hilda grabbed the last pieces of blue nettle from the ruins of her friends' exhibit and stuffed them in her pocket. "I think Trevor is planning to do something terrible," she said. "Come on, both of you. We've got to rescue that bird!"

Miss Hallgrim watched, amazed, as Hilda, David and Frida dashed out of the classroom.

"Hello?" said a voice near her elbow. "Hello? Can somebody help me?"

Miss Hallgrim stared. The voice seemed to be coming from the inside of an antique lamp.

"The sides are too slippery to climb," said the voice. "Can somebody tip me out, please? Hello?"

That was the last straw. Miss Hallgrim's eyes rolled up into her head and she fainted right there in the middle of the classroom.

The streets around the school were closed to cars and were jam-packed with chattering crowds on their way to the Bird Parade. Lots of people wore beak masks, cardboard wings and other bird-like costumes. Souvenir sellers wove their way among the crowd carrying trays of feathery key rings, raven mugs and BIRD NERD T-shirts. Strings of red and orange lanterns hung from upstairs windows.

Hilda, Frida and David joined the crowds, heading towards the marketplace. Mum had left Twig waiting outside the school and now he scampered happily at Hilda's heels, eager for adventure. As they neared the marketplace, the sound of pipes and drums grew louder and louder.

"Can you see Trevor?" Hilda shouted in David's ear.

"No!" David shouted back. "I can't see anything at all!"

It was true. The crowd was packed so tight that the three children could hardly breathe, let alone spot Trevor.

"We need stilts or something," sighed Hilda.

"I've got a better idea," said Frida. "A bell tower!"

Hilda beamed and high-fived her friend. At the top of a bell tower, they would be able to see the whole city spread out below them and would have a good chance of spotting Trevor and the raven, wherever they might be. She set off running towards the Gorrill Gardens bell tower, but Frida called her back.

"Not that tower," said Frida. "I know a better one."

Hilda and David followed Frida, ducking and diving through the crowd, hoping they were not too late. They passed the town hall and other towering buildings of inner-city Trolberg.

"In here," said Frida, pushing open a bell tower door and heading up the steps.

Hilda and Twig reached the top first and looked out over the city. A million woff-shaped lanterns twinkled like tiny night lights and there in the marketplace, beneath the muscle-bound statue of the Raven God, a line of festive floats was waiting to depart.

The music paused and an announcer spoke into a loudspeaker. "Mister Mayor, honoured guests, ladies and gentlemen, welcome to the annual

Trolberg Bird Parade. There's no sign of the Great Raven yet, but I'm sure he'll … er … be here soon."

"No, he won't," muttered Hilda. "He's trapped in a cage and he's lost his memory."

"And so, without further ado," continued the announcer, "let the parade begin!"

15

The music started up again and the line of floats moved off. People leaned out of upstairs windows and crowded on balconies to watch the spectacle. One float was shaped like an enormous bird, with people dressed as worms standing inside the beak. Another was a bluebird sitting on a nest of eggs. The school's 'Trollslayer' float was at the back of the line, chock full of excited children. Mr Magnusson had taken the place of the ruined

Edmund Ahlberg model in the middle of the float. He wore an enormous helmet that came down over his eyes.

At last, Frida and David arrived at the top of the bell tower, puffing like the Trolberg steam train. "Have you spotted Trevor yet?" panted David.

"No, it's much too dark," Hilda complained. "Unless he's on a parade float or right under a street lamp, we've got no chance of seeing him."

"In that case," said Frida, "let's shine some light on the problem, shall we?"

Hilda looked up and saw that Frida had climbed on to the pedestal of an enormous searchlight. "Wow!" gasped Hilda. "So *that's* why you chose this bell tower! Good thinking, Frida!"

Frida flicked a switch on the side of the pedestal and a powerful spotlight shone down on to the city. Frida leaned this way and that to swing the bright circle of light to and fro across the streets and alleyways of Trolberg.

"Brilliant!" cried Hilda. "Keep on doing that

and we'll give you a shout when we spot him. He's probably wearing that woolly hat of his – the orange one with the ear flaps."

"Frida," said David uncertainly. "Are you sure you're allowed to use that searchlight? I thought only the troll police were allowed to operate it."

Frida shrugged and kept on swinging the beam to and fro. "Shush, David. There's more to life than following rules, isn't that right, Hilda?"

Hilda gazed at her brave friend and for a moment she was lost for words.

"Stop staring at me!" laughed Frida. "You're supposed to be looking for Trevor."

Hilda turned back to the scene below and kept her eyes peeled for even the tiniest glimpse of orange.

"There!" cried David suddenly. "Near the church! I think that's him!"

Hilda craned her neck to look where David was pointing. Sure enough, a boy in an orange hat was sauntering along Froydis Road, swinging a cage by his side. As soon as Frida's searchlight fell on him, he started running.

"That's him!" cried Hilda. "He's heading towards the river."

"What are you waiting for?" said Frida. "I'll keep the spotlight on Trevor and you two go and rescue that poor bird."

Hilda and David hesitated. They knew that the police must already have noticed the searchlight beam and would soon be on their way to investigate.

"I'll be fine," said Frida. "Go on, RUN! You don't have much time."

Hilda was about to race back down the spiral staircase when she noticed a telephone wire running past the bell tower about two metres away. It ran to a slightly lower telegraph pole next to the post office, and then to a short pole on the corner of the marketplace. She looked at the wire and chewed her lip thoughtfully. At first glance it looked impossible, but hey, she'd done impossible before.

"Come on, Hilda," said David. "We need to go."

Hilda scooped up Twig and put him in her school bag. Then she took off her scarf and climbed up on to the railing that ran around the edge of the bell tower.

"Er – what are you doing?" asked David.

"It looks like Trevor is heading for the Bronstad Lane footbridge," said Hilda. "You approach the bridge from the west bank, David, and I'll approach from the east. We'll see if we can trap him on the bridge."

"OK," said David, "but you still haven't answered my question. What in the name of Edmund Ahlberg do you think you are doing?"

"Taking a short cut," said Hilda, and with that she reached out, looped her scarf over the telephone wire and leaped off the top of the bell tower.

David made a grab for her but caught only thin air. "YOU'RE CRAZY!" he screamed. "YOU'RE GOING TO KILL YOURSELF!"

"AAAAAAAAAAARGH!" screamed Hilda as she whizzed through the air, faster and faster. It felt like riding a speeding woff, except much harder on the arm muscles. A frightened yelp came from the bag on Hilda's back. "Sorry, Twig!" she shouted.

"I'm afraid there's a hard landing coming up!"

The post office telegraph pole came zooming towards her and – OOF! – she crashed into it chest first, knocking all the breath out of her body.

There was no time to nurse bruises. Hilda flicked her scarf free of the wire, climbed round to the other side of the pole and positioned her scarf ready for the next wire.

"AAAAAAAAAARGH!" she screamed as she raced over the roofs of Trolberg towards the marketplace. But at that moment, high above the Bird Parade, Hilda's luck ran out and her tired hands lost their grip on the scarf.

Hilda watched helplessly as her scarf slid off the telegraph wire, and the next thing she knew she was falling through the air.

"AAAAAAAAAARGH!" she screamed as she plummeted down, down, down towards the floats of the Bird Parade.

Hilda had tried her best to rescue the Great Raven and save Trolberg from famine and disaster, but her best had not been good enough. And as she looked down at the twinkling lanterns rushing up to meet her, Hilda's main feeling was sadness for the city that had become her home.

16

Sigrid Spenstig, President of Trolberg's most
popular club, stood on her float in the middle of the
Bird Parade and looked out over the merry crowd.
She preened and flapped her home-made wings,
which were made from thousands of black feathers
she had collected herself. This year's parade was
louder and more colourful than ever, but Sigrid
could not help feeling anxious. The Great Raven
had still not shown himself.

This would not be the first time the Great Raven

had forgotten to attend the Bird Parade.

When Sigrid was just eight years old, the festival ended without any appearance from the raven, and that had been a terrible year. The harvest failed, the price of food went sky high and almost everyone went hungry. It was twelve years ago, but Sigrid remembered that empty feeling in her tummy as if it was yesterday.

Sigrid looked up and scanned the night sky, hoping for a glimpse of the gigantic raven. She did not see it, but she did see something that surprised her. Something sliding down a telegraph wire above her head. And then it was no longer sliding but falling, falling, falling down towards the float.

Sigrid gasped. It was not a thing, it was a person – a little girl with blue hair and a blue school rucksack on her shoulders. Sigrid's heart missed a beat. She shut her eyes and breathed a prayer.

Hilda plunged through the air like a stone and hit the float at about thirty miles an hour. Or rather, not the actual float, but something on the float.

BOING!

Hilda felt herself bounce up into the air, then land and bounce and bounce again.

She opened her eyes. She was lying on her back on one of three enormous trampolines. A banner at the front of the float read TTC: TROLBERG TRAMPOLINING CLUB. All around her, young people in bird costumes had stopped jumping and were staring at her in amazement.

"Did you see that?" one of them said excitedly. "That girl with the blue hair just did a QUINTUPLE BACKFLIP! I thought that was impossible."

Someone else took Hilda's hand and helped her down from the trampoline. It was a young woman with short dark hair, black wings and an orange beak.

"I'm Sigrid," said the woman. "Are you OK?"

"Yes, thank you," said Hilda. "A little traumatised, but such is the life of an adventurer."

Hilda opened her school bag to let Twig out.

The deer fox lurched dizzily from side to side and fell over in a tangle of legs and antlers.

"You'll be fine in a minute," Hilda told him. "Come on, Twig, we've got to get to the river fast! Are you up for a bit of float surfing?"

Twig looked up trustingly and yipped.

Frida's beam of light was now very close to the Bronstad Lane footbridge. Hilda ran to the front of the TTC float, jumped down to the ground, ran to the next float and climbed up on to it while it was still moving.

"Hey!" said a wrinkled old man with a feather in his hat. "This is the over-eighties float. You're not over eighty, are you?"

"I have excellent skin cream," said Hilda. She dodged past him, ran to the front of the float and jumped down again.

Hilda jumped on and off six more floats, then dived down Fredrik Street, leaving the noise and the crowds far behind her. She crossed the river at Lovelock Bridge and sprinted along the east bank with Twig at her heels. Her legs ached and her breath came in short, ragged gasps, but still she ran towards the light.

A boy was walking across the Bronstad Lane footbridge, his hat and ear flaps silhouetted in the beam of Frida's searchlight.

"Oh, it's you," he said as Hilda approached. "I thought you'd be at the Bird Parade, riding on top of a stoat."

"No," said Hilda. "The only bird I'm interested in is the one you've got in that cage."

"What, this scraggly old thing?" Trevor lifted the cage and scowled at the raven inside. "The bird that talked its head off in my bedroom and then refused to say a single word at the exhibition?"

"Yes." Hilda walked forwards onto the bridge. "Give him to me, Trevor."

"Give me to her," croaked the raven.

Trevor shook his head and backed away. "You think you can beat me in a chase, Stoat Girl?"

"She doesn't need to!"

The last voice belonged to David. Hilda's heart leaped with hope as she saw her friend walk down the south bank and up on to the footbridge behind Trevor.

"You're trapped!" called David. "Give her the bird!"

Trevor turned to face him, shielding his eyes from the bright searchlight. "Is that you, Bug Head? Don't come any closer!"

"Trevor, you've already lost!" shouted Hilda. "You've got nowhere to go."

"Nowhere to go," croaked the raven.

Trevor looked from Hilda to David and from David to Hilda. "You think I've lost?" he shouted. "There's only one loser on this bridge, and it's not me!" Then he lifted the cage and spoke to the raven eye-to-eye. "I'm sorry, Birdy. I'm afraid the loser's you."

"NO!" shrieked Hilda, running forward.

But it was too late. Trevor swung the birdcage as hard as he could and let it go. Cage and raven

sailed through the air, over the parapet of the bridge and down into the deep river.

Hilda rushed to the edge of the bridge and looked down. Nothing. The cage had sunk without trace. Hilda kicked off her boots and took a deep breath.

"Don't!" cried David.

But Hilda had already dived off the bridge into the dark, swirling water below.

17

When she had lived in the wilderness with Mum, Hilda had often gone swimming in the catfish pool near her house. Every summer she had practised diving down to the bottom of the pool and holding her breath for as long as possible. Little did she know that she would one day need those skills at the bottom of a freezing cold river in Trolberg.

It was pitch black under water, but Hilda kept calm and swam down to the river bed with long powerful strokes. She dolphin kicked to and fro

until at last her fingers touched the cold metal bars
of a birdcage. She lifted the latch. She felt around
inside the cage. She grabbed the cold, limp bird.
But when she tried to kick towards the surface,
she realised she was stuck. A clump of knotweed
was twisted around her ankle and the more she
tried to shake it free the more tangled up she got.

Hilda could not hold her breath much longer.
If you really are the Great Raven, she thought,
now would be a good time to remember that!

Fighting back the urge to breathe, she took
the blue nettle from her pocket and pushed a single
leaf into the raven's beak. The raven chewed
and swallowed.

In her short life Hilda had talked with giants,
run from battle bunnies and had an elf cat give
birth in her hair. But what happened next was
the most amazing thing she had ever experienced.
She felt the raven swell and rise and suddenly –
WHUMP! – the bird was out of her hands, gigantic
in her outstretched arms. As Hilda held on tight

to those massive chest feathers, the tangled knotweed tore off at the roots and up they shot together, bird and girl, rocketing to the surface of the water and out into the glorious night air.

"I REMEMBER EVERYTHING!" the raven cawed.

Hilda opened wide her mouth and filled her lungs with cool, sweet Trolberg air. She caught a glimpse of Trevor and David in the beam of the searchlight, two upturned faces slack with awe. Hilda could only imagine their astonishment as they watched their classmate burst out of the rushing river on the back of a colossal bird.

The bird soared over the city with Hilda on his back. Higher and higher they flew.

"I was right!" Hilda cried. "You ARE the Great Raven!"

"No, I'm not," said the bird.

"What?"

"It was all a big misunderstanding. Many years ago I was passing over Trolberg and decided to take a break on that statue in the marketplace. When the harvest turned out well that year, the townspeople thought it was my doing and they started the annual Bird Parade."

"I don't get it," said Hilda. "If you're not the Great Raven, why do you bother turning up at the Bird Parade each year?"

"The parade is in my honour," said the bird. "It would be rude not to show up. As it happens, there was one year when I had bird flu and couldn't come. The people of Trolberg got so depressed that year, they didn't bother working in their fields. The harvest was terrible, of course."

"I see," said Hilda. "So, if you're not the Great Raven, what are you?"

"I'm a thunderbird."

"What's that?"

"I'll show you."

The thunderbird raised his wings and cawed at the top of his voice. A bolt of lightning forked across the night sky with an ear-splitting thunderclap.

"Wow," said Hilda.

The thunder and lightning attracted the attention of the people below. The loudspeaker in the marketplace crackled into life.

"He's HERE!" the announcer exclaimed. "The Great Raven is here! Restart the parade!"

The huge woff lanterns had been snuffed out all over Trolberg, but they were quickly relit and the city twinkled once again. Pipes and drums began to play. People clapped and whooped for joy while Frida swung the searchlight onto the giant bird, highlighting him for all to see.

"Hold on tight," said the bird and Hilda performed her second quintuple somersault of the night, this time on the back of a magical thunderbird.

"I'm on top of the WORLD!" yelled Hilda, laughing.

After a few more fly-pasts and a dozen loop-the-loops, the thunderbird flew lower so that Hilda could look out for her mum.

"There she is!" cried Hilda. "She's sitting

on that high wall near the train station, right where she said she'd be."

The bird swooped down and landed silently on the roof of the train station.

"Goodbye, Great Raven," said Hilda, wriggling off his back.

"Goodbye, Zelda," said the thunderbird. "Thanks for everything." With that, he lifted his head, flapped his powerful black wings and flew away into the night sky.

Hilda slithered down a drainpipe and landed on the wall next to her mum.

"Hi, Mum," she said.

"Hilda!" exclaimed Mum, hugging her tight. "I've been waiting for you. Where did you and your friends dash off to?"

"I'll tell you later," smiled Hilda. "Look, the parade is coming!"

As the festival floats turned into Station Road, the people lining the street suddenly burst out singing, and Hilda's heart was filled with

boundless delight.

"I used to come and sit here to watch the parade when I was your age," said Mum. "It's my favourite day of the year."

"Mine too," said Hilda.

The people walking alongside the floats were wearing all sorts of weird and wonderful costumes. Dresses with huge puffed sleeves. Bird-themed hats of every sort. Cardboard beaks held on with elastic. Feathery eyelashes. Hilda even saw a sausage dog dressed up as a bird.

"Oh, by the way," said Mum, reaching into her handbag. "Alfur has been asking for you." She reached into her bag and took out an old clay lamp.

"Hello?" said a tetchy voice. "Hilda, is that you?"

Hilda grabbed the lamp and tipped it up. Out slid an angry elf.

"Thanks for abandoning me!" yelled Alfur. "I lost count of the number of people who stepped on me, before your mum spotted me."

Hilda giggled. "Look on the bright side," she said, putting the elf back in her ear. "If you'd been with me, you'd have had a very cold plunge in the River Björg."

"Ugh." Alfur shivered. "Perhaps the lamp wasn't so bad, after all."

Mother and daughter sat on the train station wall, swinging their legs and watching the parade. The over-eighties float went past, full of wrinkly white-haired birds. The trampoline float followed, radiant ravens flying high. Sigrid noticed Hilda mid-jump and gave her a happy wave.

The school float brought up the rear of the parade. Mr Magnusson was now waving a floppy cardboard sword. Frida and David were on the float as well. They did not see her, but boy, was Hilda glad to see them. Their adventures together had certainly been *trol-matic*, but Hilda had a feeling that she and Frida and David would be friends for life.

"Wonderful," said Hilda out loud.

Mum turned to look at her. "What is, darling?"

"All of it," said Hilda. "The city. The people. The crazy feather costumes. It's all wonderful."

Mum put her arm around Hilda's shoulder and pulled her close. "I'm glad you think so," she whispered.

IN THE NEXT BOOK...

Hilda has joined the Sparrow Scouts and is eager to impress her mum by earning plenty of badges. Although her first twelve attempts haven't gone well, Hilda is as optimistic as ever and determined to at least get her camping badge before the Badge Ceremony.

But of course, the life of an adventurer is rarely simple. Not only must Hilda cope with a self-loathing giant, a bloodthirsty hound and a homeless house spirit – she must also get to grips with the mindboggling science of Nowhere Space.